The Remarkable Pencils

Contents

The Boy 2

The Boy's Drawing 6

The Tiny Folk 10

Tiny Land 14

The Girl 17

The Attack 20

The Girl's Drawing 24

The Meeting 26

The Real World Again. 29

Now 32

Written and Illustrated by
Anton Petrov

The Boy

Once upon a time, there was a boy who loved to draw. From as far back as he could remember he had always loved drawing. When he was very young he drew squiggles. He drew his squiggles every day, and sometimes he drew them in places he shouldn't, like on the kitchen wall or in a book. Then his mother would scold him.

"Did you do that?" she would ask angrily. Then the boy would start to cry because he knew that walls were not for drawing on.

"Don't ever do that again," his mother would scold. "You have plenty of paper to draw your pictures on and that's the only place you can draw − on your paper! Do you hear me?"

The boy would nod in agreement and draw on paper until he forgot again and drew in a book or on the floor. Then his mother would tell him that if he did it again she would take his crayons away from him. But she never did.

Everyone said that the little boy's drawings were just squiggles, but the boy knew that they were really magnificent pictures. It was just that his hands couldn't quite make the pictures that he could see in his head.

"This is a picture of me going to school on my very first day," he would say proudly. Or, "This is a rocket ship going to the space station." In response, the grown-ups would just nod and smile indulgently and say nothing.

As he grew older, the boy's drawings became more recognizable to other people. He started to draw things that looked very real, such as the sky, the sun, trees, houses, and people. Then everyone said, "That's a lovely picture of an airport." Or, "Ooh, that's really good. You'll be an excellent artist one day, that's for sure."

The boy was very happy. His parents loved him and his grandfather visited often, bringing presents. For his 11th birthday, the boy received a present from his grandfather – a brand new set of pencils. The boy was very happy. But he was not as happy as he would have been if his present had been a bike or a skateboard or a video game. Just because he liked to draw didn't mean that he wanted to draw all the time. And anyway, he already had various different sets of pencils that his parents and their friends had given him over the years. Those sets had dozens of different pencils in them. But this one only had seven – red, orange, yellow, green, blue, violet, and brown. The most unusual thing was, there was no black pencil. All of his other pencil sets had black pencils.

"Why isn't there a black pencil in this set?" the boy asked his grandfather. "Do you think it was left out on purpose?"

"Well, I have no idea," replied his grandfather. "How strange. Perhaps it fell out in the store. But not to worry, I'm sure you already have lots of black pencils."

The Boy's Drawing

A couple of weeks after his grandfather had brought the present, the boy decided to draw a picture with his new pencils. He started to draw people, planes, trees, and the sun. He worked incredibly hard. The drawing took him a long time because he put in a lot of detail. But as he drew, he felt that there was something very unusual about this drawing. He felt as if the pencils were drawing the picture by themselves. When he had finished, he was very excited about how his picture looked. It was one of the best pictures he had ever drawn. "It's a masterpiece!" he thought.

The people looked so lifelike he felt like striking up conversations with them. Some of the people were old, bent, and wrinkled, and some of them were exuberant and young. Some were short and some were tall. Some were thin as pins, and others looked like roly-poly dumplings. They had different skin tones and different types of hair.

The trees the boy drew seemed like they were really growing. He could imagine them changing from green to red to bronze and then the wind tearing off their leaves to carpet the ground as the summer ended. He could also almost believe that the planes were really taking off from the airports. He could almost hear the roar of the jets as they soared into the blue sky.

The boy felt warm looking at his picture. He didn't know whether it was because he felt so good about it or because he really could feel the heat of the fiery golden sun.

The boy grabbed his drawing and rushed down the wooden stairs to show it to his parents. But then an unusual thing happened. When his parents looked at the sheet of paper, it was as empty and white as a clean sheet.

"Are you trying to trick us?" his father asked with a twinkle in his eye.

"What did you draw a picture of?" asked his mother, trying to keep a straight face.

The boy was surprised and confused. The sheet of paper on which he had drawn his best-ever picture had absolutely nothing on it. It was completely blank. Where had his picture gone?

"I definitely drew it," he said to his parents. "It's not a trick picture. In fact, it was the best picture I've ever drawn. I must have picked up the wrong piece of paper." But he knew in his heart of hearts that he hadn't. He shook his head, mystified.

"What happened?" the boy said to himself as he walked back up the stairs to his room carrying the blank sheet of paper. He checked all the other pieces of paper, but they were blank, too, just as he knew they would be. He had definitely drawn his picture on the paper he had taken to show his parents. The boy sat down at the table and stared at the paper for a long, long time. "Was I just dreaming that I drew a picture?" he said to himself.

The Tiny Folk

"Be careful! Watch out! Oh no!" someone screamed in a tiny voice from the floor beside the table where the boy was sitting. The boy looked down and there on the carpet he saw some tiny people running around in a panic. They looked exactly like the people he had just drawn. The people were running between higgledy-piggledy trees, some of which had fallen over and some of which were still standing.

"Those are the trees I drew," the boy said, astonished. Between the trees there was an airstrip and some planes were trying, unsuccessfully, to take off. Then the boy noticed a shining sun that gave off so much heat he could feel it on his bare feet.

"That has to be the picture that I just drew," he said to himself. "What on earth is going on? I must be dreaming. Am I awake or asleep?" And he pinched himself hard on the back of his hand to find out the answer.

"Ouch!" the boy shouted. "I guess I must be awake!"

"This boy is the clumsiest I've ever seen," shouted one of the tiny people from the floor as she scurried out of the way of a falling tree.

"He should show us some respect," shouted another tiny person angrily, as he dodged a wayward branch.

"Yeah, throwing us down like that. I ask you, what next?" said a tiny woman with three very tiny children.

"Just horrible," they all agreed, nodding their little heads.

The boy, astounded, got down on his knees to take a closer look at what was going on. "Who are you, and what's wrong?" he asked them.

"You have the nerve to ask us what's wrong?" screeched one of the older tiny folk. "You're the one to blame. Didn't you see us

11

fall off the paper when you rushed out to show your parents your drawing?"

"Fall off the paper! How could you fall off the paper?" asked the boy, beginning to believe that he really must be dreaming and pinching his hand again to make sure he wasn't.

"So you drew us and you don't even recognize us," replied the tiny woman indignantly. "Remember, not an hour ago you created us and we were so lifelike you thought you could even talk to us."

"Oh, I really am sorry," said the boy, "but nothing I've ever drawn has fallen off the paper and come to life before."

12

"Well, that's because you've never drawn with remarkable pencils before," said the tiny woman knowingly. "This time you used remarkable pencils and you created our world."

"Oh," said the boy, still not quite sure what was going on. Then he remembered his manners and introduced himself.

"I'm William," he said. "Do you folks have names, too?"

"Not that we know of," snapped a wrinkly and very grumpy old man. "You drew us. Why don't you name us?"

So William thought up as many names as he could and gave them to the tiny people.

"OK, you can be Caleb, and you can be Minh, and you can  be Yianna," he said, pointing to the three small folk nearest to him. "And you can be Stavros, and you can be Sergio, and you can be Serafina," he continued. "Oh dear. I don't think I can remember any more than that," he said. "I'll do the rest later."

Tiny Land

"Well, what are you going to do now?" asked the grumpy old man that William had named Caleb. "It's not good enough just to give us names. You could go off now and forget all about us."

"I think I'll just put you all back onto the paper," William replied. "Then I'll finish my drawing." With that, he very carefully gathered up all the little people. Then he gathered up the trees and the sun. Last of all he gathered up the planes and the airstrip. He put them all back on his paper where they belonged. Then he picked up his remarkable pencils and began to draw some more.

"I wonder what would happen if I drew myself into the picture?" William thought. Then without any delay he started to draw himself. But before he had even finished drawing his left leg, he began to feel different. He noticed that he was now inside the drawing and everything he drew was as real as in ordinary life. He drew birds that sang and flowers that smelled like perfume. Then he drew all kinds of animals that ran, crawled, and flew busily around. Lastly, he drew a whole town full of buildings.

The tiny folk were ecstatic and they all began to talk at once. They jumped up and down and hugged each other and began singing and dancing. They welcomed William like a king and prepared a big feast to celebrate. So William drew chocolate cakes, fruit pies, and lemonade. Then he drew fireworks that shot up into the sky like a million dancing glowworms. He drew musicians who played the sweetest melodies he had ever heard. It was one spectacular party!

Everyone was having a great time when suddenly some ugly black dots appeared in the sky, growing bigger and bigger as they got closer.

"What is it?" screamed a tiny girl.

"Are they thunderbolts?" asked the tiny woman called Minh.

"What shall we do?" they cried, looking to William for guidance.

"Quick! Run and hide!" shouted William. So the tiny folk stumbled and tumbled over each other as they fled into the trees, desperate for shelter from the menacing alien objects that were approaching fast.

The Girl

Once upon a time, there was a girl. She was 12 years old and lived with her aunt in a small apartment that was bare and damp. The paint was peeling from the walls and the windows didn't fasten properly so that it was always too cold in the winter and too hot in the summer.

To make ends meet, the girl's aunt worked long hours, often late into the night, which meant that, most of the time, the girl was on her own. In the morning, the girl got herself up and got dressed for school long before her aunt was out of bed. Then she caught the school bus that stopped near the apartment. After school each day, the girl played with the children who lived nearby. Then, as it got dark and her friends returned to their own homes for dinner, she arrived back at the empty apartment and watched TV. Because there was not much money, there was not much food to eat, so the girl was often hungry. As well as that, she was always lonely, always sad, and sometimes very very angry.

One day after school had finished, the girl went to play with her friends as usual. For a while they played jump-rope games in front of the apartment building. Then they played video games at another girl's house. After everyone else had gone home to have dinner and do their homework, the girl wandered aimlessly along the street. She didn't really want to go back to the apartment that night. She was tired of all the hours she spent by herself. Right then, she felt more alone than she ever had before.

Suddenly, just where she was about to step, the girl saw a black pencil on the ground. It looked like an ordinary black pencil, but for some reason the girl felt compelled to bend down and pick it up. "I'm sure the owner won't bother to look for it," she said to herself, as the sun began to disappear below the horizon. So the girl put the pencil in her pocket and took it home.

"I wonder if I could draw," she thought to herself as she let herself into the dark apartment and turned on the light. But she had no paper to draw on, so she put the thought out of her mind. She ate dinner and then watched TV until her eyes were so heavy she could no longer keep them open. She went to her room, took the pencil out of her pocket, and put it under her pillow so she wouldn't lose it. Immediately, she dropped into a deep dark sleep.

Two weeks passed by and the girl's lonely life continued on as usual. She got up, went to school, played with friends, and then came home to her empty home. At night, she watched TV until she was tired and then went to bed. She still had not used the pencil. But every evening when she came into the apartment she took it out from under her pillow and held it while she watched TV. When she went to bed, she tucked it under her pillow again. Somehow she felt attached to the pencil as though it was a friend.

Then, on the last day of the week, the girl brought some paper home from school to finish a science project. She struggled with the project by herself because there was no one to help her. As she struggled, she got angrier and angrier until at last she picked up the black pencil and drew large black circles all over the paper. Then she furiously filled in the outlines she had made, going over and over the black, pressing as hard as she could. Then she drew thick black lines over and through the circles. She drew and she drew and she drew until the paper was completely covered with black lines and circles. She vented all her frustration and all her rage on the paper. Finally, when all her anger was spent, she threw the pencil on the floor and began to sob uncontrollably.

The Attack

Back in Tiny Land, the tiny folk had been thrown into confusion. They ran helter-skelter, this way and that. There was mayhem everywhere as the people ran frantically in all directions looking for places that might provide some shelter.

"Don't panic!" shouted William. "It's probably just a temporary electrical disturbance." But to everybody's horror, the dots were getting bigger and blacker as they approached.

"What is it?" screamed the people again and again as they crouched down trying to avoid the oncoming disaster. "We've never seen anything like this before."

Then, as William tried desperately to think of an explanation for what was going on, other things started appearing in the sky. On top of the big black spots were streaks of black lightning and although the streaks were silent, the people were more petrified than they would have been in the most ferocious thunderstorm.

"We're being invaded," screamed Yianna. "We'll all be killed. There's no way we can escape!" Her panic was contagious and soon screams were pouring out of hundreds of mouths like a huge avalanche of sound.

William was frightened, too. He couldn't imagine what would happen if any of these fierce-looking lines and spots touched down. He hoped that they would just move across the sky or dissipate before they got any closer. But suddenly, as they got closer, they were no longer silent. The noise, like huge sobs, was deafening, almost unbearable. William tried to muffle it by clapping his hands over his ears.

"Cover your ears!" he screamed to the tiny folk as the noise got louder and louder. Then, for what seemed like forever, William and the tiny folk cowered in the shelter of the trees with their ears covered, watching the anger in the sky.

Eventually, William had a thought. "I'm the only one who can stop this certain destruction," he said to himself. "I'm the only one who can find out what's causing this devastation, but first I need to stop it before everyone is dead."

So he got out his remarkable pencils and drew. He drew a huge cannon shooting brilliant lights in all directions. As the lights exploded from the cannon and splashed on the black shapes, their fury seemed to dissipate. As new black objects appeared, William shot more lights at them and he kept on shooting his brilliant

cannonballs until no more objects appeared. In the end, the only things left were huge raindrops falling like tears onto Tiny Land.

When the rain finally stopped, the still-nervous tiny folk came out of their hiding places to thank William.

"Thank you, thank you," they said. "Without you, we would all be dead. But how do we know that it won't happen again?"

"We don't," replied William. Then, with a flash of insight, he said, "But I think I know how this disaster happened. I think it has something to do with the missing black pencil."

The Girl's Drawing

The girl sat in front of her drawing, her anger slowly subsiding as the tears came. A flood of tears washed down onto the paper and she cried and cried until it seemed she had no more tears to cry. Then she picked up the pencil and took it to her bedroom, where she fell asleep.

The next day, the girl decided to go straight home from school and draw again. This time she decided to see if she could draw herself. First she looked in the mirror to see what she really looked like. Then she took the black pencil and began the outline. She started with an oval for her face. Then she added her eyes, her nose, and a sad mouth that drooped down at the corners. She finished her head by covering her ears with bunches of tight corkscrew curls. Next she drew her body, which was thin, with legs that were too long and feet that were too big.

As she drew she started to feel sad, lonely, and sorry for herself, so she left the drawing and went to watch TV while she waited for her aunt to arrive home.

"Have you been watching TV since you got home from school?" asked her aunt disapprovingly when she returned.

"No. I've been doing my homework and I've been drawing," replied the girl. "I found a black pencil on the street and I drew a picture of myself – I'll show you if you want," she said, racing off to her room to get the drawing.

"What do you mean, drawing?" asked her aunt in a surprised voice when the girl returned with the picture. "There's no drawing on this paper at all. It's blank. Are you trying to trick me?"

"No, I'm not trying to trick you," the girl replied, taking the paper from her aunt. But sure enough, the page was blank. The picture she had drawn of herself had completely vanished. "I guess I fell asleep and just dreamed it all," the girl thought as she went back to her room. "Maybe I can't draw at all."

The Meeting

"Someone must have the missing remarkable pencil," William told the tiny folk. "That person is full of anger and sadness. That's why they're drawing pictures full of darkness and destruction."

"You mean it was a drawing that attacked us?" asked Yianna, looking at William with amazement. "How can that be?"

"Remember, it was me who drew you with my remarkable pencils," replied William. "And then I drew myself into the picture and that's how I came to be here. Now someone else has drawn a picture using the missing black pencil."

"But what can you do about this catastrophe?" asked Sergio.

"If I knew who the person was, I could get the pencil back," replied William. "That would stop it. But I don't have a clue who the person is or where the person lives."

"Why don't you draw a door?" suggested Serafina. "You could write a message on the door."

"Yes, William," said Yianna. "Draw a gigantic front door."

"That's a good idea," said William, and he drew a front door with the green pencil. Then he wrote in large red letters, *The door to the house of the person who has the black pencil.*

Just as he finished the picture, a sad-looking girl opened the door and walked through it into Tiny Land.

"Oh no!" one of the tiny folk exclaimed as they all backed away, not taking their eyes off the unexpected intruder.

"Who are you, and what is this place?" the girl asked, looking around in wide-eyed amazement.

Before anyone could reply, Caleb, the grumpy old man, found some courage and shouted, "Are you the person who's been trying to wreck our land and kill us all with your horrible pictures? Are you the one who drew those dreadful black spots and lines?"

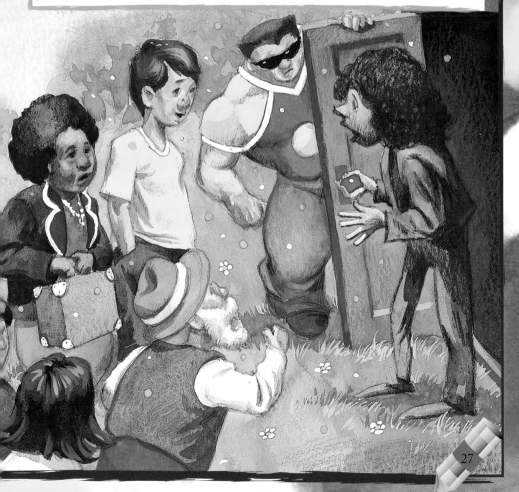

The girl didn't answer, and when William moved closer to her, he saw that she was crying silently.

"You must be the person who has my black pencil," he said kindly. "What's your name, and why are you so unhappy?"

"I'm Juliana," replied the girl as the tears trickled in rivulets down her cheeks and dripped from her chin onto the ground. "I found a pencil in the street and I drew a picture with it, a mean, ugly picture. I drew it because I was sad and lonely and angry. Later, I drew a picture of myself, but when I showed it to my aunt, the paper was completely blank. I couldn't understand it."

"That explains it," said William to himself. "You disappeared from your drawing because the pencil you used to draw your pictures is remarkable," he said to Juliana. "You got here because you drew yourself and then you fell off the paper when you picked the picture up to show your aunt."

"I did what?" Juliana answered, her tears subsiding.

"That's how I got here," continued William. "I drew Tiny Land and then it fell off my paper. So I drew myself and now I'm here. I drew the door that you just came through and that's how you got here."

"But why do you want to destroy our beautiful land?" persisted Caleb, staring furiously at Juliana.

"I don't want to destroy your land," replied Juliana, starting to cry again. "I didn't know anything like that was happening. As I told you, I was just upset and lonely and angry."

The Real World Again

"Don't cry, Juliana," said William sympathetically. "If you found the pencil on the street, it might mean that you live near my grandpa. He lives on his own and he sometimes feels lonely, too. Maybe you can come with me when I visit him. And when we're there we could draw some pictures together."

"That would be wonderful," said Juliana, her face erupting into a smile through the last of her tears.

"Good idea," said Caleb. "We don't want you drawing those catastrophic pictures again. We were all terrified we were going to be killed. Next time you reach boiling point, if William isn't here to draw us out of danger, we might not be so lucky. Next time, draw some joyful and inspirational pictures."

"Yes, but first we have to draw something practical," William said to Juliana. "I have the rest of the pencils with me. Together, we'll draw a picture that takes us back to the real world. You draw your house and I'll draw my grandpa's. Then we'll draw the streets around the houses and see if they match up. You draw yourself on the street where you found the pencil and I'll draw myself outside my grandpa's house."

So that's what they did. Together, William and Juliana

collaborated on a picture that took them back into the real world.

"You were right, William," said Juliana, as they met on the path outside William's grandpa's house. "I do live close to your grandpa. This is exactly where I found the black pencil. Your grandpa must have dropped it."

"Grandpa's not home right now," said William, noticing that his grandpa's car wasn't there. "So why don't you come to my house? I've got an assortment of pencils at home and different kinds of paper, too. You can have some of them to draw with. I'll introduce you to my parents, then I'll take you to meet my grandpa later."

Juliana accompanied William to his house and that turned into the first of many visits. William also introduced Juliana to his grandpa. After that, with her aunt's permission, Juliana dropped in to visit him after school sometimes. Mostly, though, Juliana spent her free time drawing and she became so good at it that after a while she couldn't imagine a time when she hadn't known how to draw.

Now

William and Juliana are both grown up and leading busy lives now. William has left home and works as the manager of a large publishing company that specializes in books for children. On his office wall is a drawing he did of the attack on Tiny Land. He looks at the drawing every day and it reminds him that there are people in the world who are sad and lonely and not as fortunate as he is.

Juliana is now a teacher, teaching art to students who have serious disabilities. She has never forgotten the time when she was a sad, lonely, angry child. Juliana tries to help children express themselves through their drawings so that they never feel as bad as she used to.

Juliana and William still see each other as often as they can. Sometimes they go to the movies together, sometimes they go hiking or biking, and sometimes they collaborate on a drawing or painting project.

The remarkable pencils are all together in a special box. William and Juliana take turns looking after them, but they never, ever use them now.